RODDY DOYLE

MAD WEEKEND

Roddy Doyle has written eight novels, including *Paddy Clarke Ha Ha Ha* (1993), *The Woman Who Walked Into Doors* (1996) and, most recently, *Paula Spencer* (2006). He wrote a memoir of his parents, *Rory and Ita* (2002). He has written three books for children, including *The Giggler Treatment* (2000). He has also written for stage, screen and television.

All royalties from the Irish sales of the Open Door series go to a charity of the author's choice. *Mad Weekend* royalties go to Kilbarrack Community Development Project, c/o St Mary's National School, Swan's Nest Road, Dublin 5.

NEW ISLAND *Open Door*

MAD WEEKEND
First published 2006
by New Island
2 Brookside
Dundrum Road
Dublin 14

www.newisland.ie

A CIP catalogue record for this book is available from the British Library

ISBN 1 905494 04 1

New Island receives financial assistance from
The Arts Council (An Chomhairle Ealaíon), Dublin, Ireland.

Typeset by New Island
Printed in Ireland by ColourBooks
Cover design by Artmark

1 3 5 4 2

Dear Reader,

On behalf of myself and the other contributing authors, I would like to welcome you to the fifth Open Door series. We hope that you enjoy the books and that reading becomes a lasting pleasure in your life.

Warmest wishes,

Patricia Scanlan.

Patricia Scanlan
Series Editor

One

This is a true story. It's about men and football and drink. So it must be true.

There were three men. They were young. There were all twenty when the story starts. Dave, Pat and Ben. They had been friends since they were kids. They went to the same school. They played for the same football team. They drank their first beer from the same bottle. Dave and Pat even got their first kiss from the same girl. Ben didn't, because the girl was his sister. But that's another story.

So. Dave, Pat and Ben were best friends. They were The Lads. They were always together. They went to the same films. They went to the same pubs and clubs.

Once, they even broke their noses on the same night. They were on the last bus home. They were upstairs, in the front seats. A dog ran onto the street. The driver put his foot on the brake. Dave, Pat and Ben hit the window at the same time. Bang, bang and bang.

They loved the same music. They followed the same team.

Liverpool.

And that's where the story starts.

Two

The story doesn't start *in* Liverpool. It starts in Dublin. In a pub in Dublin. It starts on 25 May 2005. It starts two seconds after Liverpool won the European Cup. Two seconds after the Liverpool goal-keeper saved the last penalty.

The story starts like this.

'Yes!'

'Yes!'

'Yes!'

Dave jumped onto the table. Ben jumped up beside him. Pat was up there already.

'Yes!'

The pub was full of noise. The place was full of Liverpool fans. They were cheering. They were laughing. They were hugging and crying.

In the yard behind the pub, two Liverpool fans were having sex.

By the way, one of them was a woman.

'If it's a boy we'll call him Stevie!'

'Yes, yes. Don't stop! What if it's a girl?'

'Oh, God. We'll call her Stevie too.'

'What if it's twins?'

'Two Stevies!'

Back in the pub, the lads were still up on the table. They sang.

'Who let the Reds out! Woof, woof, woof, woof, woof!'

They watched the telly. They saw Stevie Gerrard, the Liverpool captain, pick up the cup and kiss it. The cup was huge. He lifted it over his head.

The lads cheered. The whole pub cheered.

Pat put his leg out. The table wasn't there.

'Where's the table?'

He fell. He was holding Ben. Ben fell too. Ben was holding Dave. They all fell. They were covered in Guinness and Heineken. They didn't care.

'Who let the Reds out! Woof, woof, woof, woof, woof!'

The lads sat up.

'My arse is wet,' said Pat.

'We won,' said Dave. 'That's worth a damp arse.'

They got up off the floor.

'We weren't even born the last time they won the European Cup,' said Ben.

'We'll go to Liverpool next year,' said Dave.

'Yes,' said Pat. 'For a match.'

'Cool,' said Ben. 'For the weekend.'

'It will be great, man,' said Dave.

And *that's* the start of the story.

Three

It was four months later. The summer was over. The football had started again.

It was Saturday morning. The lads were at the airport. They were flying to Liverpool. It was very early in the morning. It was very, very early. It was six o'clock.

Dave was on the floor. His bag was his pillow. He was trying to sleep.

But Ben wouldn't let Dave sleep. Ben was nervous. He had never been in a plane. This was his first time.

It was always the same. Ben was the nervous one.

Pat slept. Dave tried to sleep. Ben stayed wide awake. He kicked Dave. Not very hard.

'It's still yesterday, man,' said Dave. 'Go away.'

'I can't wait for the match,' said Ben.

'Go away,' said Dave.

Dave shut his eyes.

Ben kicked Pat. But Pat didn't wake up. He was lying across three seats. Ben kicked him again. A little bit harder. Pat didn't wake up. Ben kicked him hard.

Pat woke up.

'Are we there yet?' he said.

He saw that they were still at the airport and he went back to sleep.

There were other Liverpool fans there. Some awake, some asleep.

Ben was nervous. He looked out at the plane. It looked big. It looked safe. But up in the air it would be very small.

The wind would throw it all over the place.

Just in case you think this story is going to be about a plane crash, it's not.

The lads got on the plane. The plane took off. It flew to Liverpool, no problem, and it landed. It took thirty minutes.

But what Ben did on the plane is a big part of the story. He drank a load of whiskey. Dave and Pat were asleep. They didn't see Ben drinking.

When they got off the plane at Liverpool Airport, Ben was drunk. It was ten past seven in the morning.

Four

Ben was drunk. But he wasn't very drunk. He wasn't sick or stupid. He was fine.

He was very happy.

'We're still alive,' he said.

He got down on his knees. He kissed the floor of the airport.

'Hello, Liverpool,' he said.

'Get up, you muppet,' said Dave.

They were all laughing. It was a good start to the day.

They got a taxi to the hotel. Dave sat beside the driver. Ben and Pat sat in the back.

Dave sniffed the air.

'There was someone drinking whiskey in this taxi last night,' he said.

'I wasn't working last night,' said the driver.

'Well, someone was drinking, man,' said Dave. 'Can you smell it?' he asked.

'Yes,' said Pat.

'No,' said Ben.

They arrived at the hotel. They paid the driver and got out of the taxi.

'I think the driver was drunk,' said Dave. 'There was a smell of whiskey off him.'

Ben said nothing.

They booked into the hotel. They went up to their room. They counted the beds.

'One, two, three,' said Pat. 'That's grand.'

Dave opened the wardrobe door. He looked in.

'There's loads of room for the women,' he said.

They laughed. They threw their bags on the beds.

'Let's go,' said Dave.

'Breakfast,' said Pat.

'Excellent,' said Dave.

They went to the door.

'Hang on,' said Dave. 'There's a smell of whiskey in here too.'

He sniffed.

'Do you smell it?' said Dave.

'No,' said Ben.

'Yes,' said Pat.

They went out. They walked for a bit. It was still very early. It was very quiet. All the shops were shut. But they came to a café that was open. They went in.

'What'll we have?' said Dave.

'The full Irish,' said Pat.

'We're in England, you muppet,' said Dave.

Ben laughed.

'Hang on,' said Dave. 'That whiskey smell is back.'

He sniffed his jacket. He sniffed his hands. People were looking at him. He sniffed under his arms.

Ben laughed again.

'I can smell it too,' said Pat.

He was sitting beside Ben. He sniffed Ben.

'It's you,' he said.

'Lay off,' said Ben. 'It is not.'

'It is,' said Pat. 'I can smell it.'

'Okay,' said Ben.

He put his hands in the air.

'It's me.'

'When did you drink?' said Dave.

He looked at the clock on his mobile phone.

'It's only eight o'clock,' he said.

'I had a bottle on the plane,' said Ben. 'For my nerves.'

'You drank a whole bottle?'

'No,' said Ben. 'Just a few sips.'

'You smell like a Christmas pudding,' said Pat.

'I'm grand,' said Ben.

'Are you drunk?' said Dave.

'Not at all,' said Ben. 'Come on. Breakfast. I'm starving.'

They had eggs, rashers, sausages, more eggs, toast, tea, chocolate cake and a few eggs.

'That was great,' said Pat.

He thumped his stomach.

'Are the pubs open yet?' said Ben.

Dave looked at his mobile.

'It's half-eight,' he said. 'And you're drunk already.'

'I'm not,' said Ben. 'I feel great.'

They went walking again. They walked down to the river. They sat beside it. The river was very wide and the waves looked great in the sun.

Ben was looking into the water.

'Are you okay?' said Dave.

'I'm fine,' said Ben.

'Are you going to get sick?' said Dave.

'No.'

'You look very white.'

'I am white,' said Ben. 'My ma and da are white. So I'm white. That's the way it happens, Dave.'

'Okay,' said Dave.

'Let me know if I turn black, Dave,' said Ben.

'Shut up, Ben,' said Dave.

'Let's get the boat,' said Pat.

'Good idea.'

The boat was a ferry. It crossed the river every ten minutes or so. The lads could see the ferry coming near.

They got tickets and walked onto the ferry. It went back on the river. The waves were big and a bit mad. The

ferry went over them, up and down, up
– and – down.

Pat and Dave held on to the rail.
They looked at Ben. He was looking
down at the water.

'Okay, Ben?'

'Yes.'

'Are you going to get sick?'

'No.'

'Sure?'

'Yes.'

'Cross your heart and hope to die?'

'Piss off, Dave.'

The ferry went up and down.

'All right there, Ben?'

'Piss off,' said Ben.

'How is the breakfast?'

'Piss off.'

'The rashers were lovely,' said Dave.

'Piss off.'

'And the fat on the rashers.'

'Piss off.'

'And the eggs,' said Pat. 'They were lovely and yellow and runny.'

'Piss off,' said Ben.

'Yum yum.'

'Piss off.'

Ben didn't get sick. But when they got off the ferry his face was very, very white. He sat on the ground. He put his face in his hands.

Dave looked at the clock on his mobile.

'The pubs are open,' he said.

'Oh God,' said Ben.

Five

They walked back into the centre of the city. Ben was okay again. He was still a white Irish man but he didn't look like a sick white Irish man.

'I'll take it easy,' he said.

'Good man,' said Dave.

'I'll only have one pint before the match,' said Ben.

'Good idea,' said Dave.

The shops were open. There were people on the streets. There were people in Liverpool jerseys. The sun was out. The girls were out. The jackets were off.

'This is the life,' said Pat.

'This is the pub,' said Dave.

They were at the pub they had been looking for. It was called the Bee Hive. They had been told that this was the best pub in Liverpool. 'You have to go there,' they'd been told. 'It's mad.'

The lads looked at the pub. It didn't look mad.

'It looks dead,' said Ben.

'Let's go in,' said Dave.

'Ladies first,' said Pat.

Dave pushed the door. He went in. Pat went in. Ben followed them.

They stood there.

It was like a room in a granny's house.

'Jesus,' said Pat.

There was granny wallpaper and granny pictures on the walls. There were black and white photos of old film stars. There was a jukebox and music.

Tom Jones was singing 'The Green Green Grass of Home'.

'Will you listen to that crap?' said Ben.

The smell of old drink was making him sick again.

'Who told you that this place was great?' said Pat.

'My ma,' said Dave.

'Your ma?'

'And my da,' said Dave. 'But other people as well. They all said it was great.'

Tom Jones stopped singing.

'Thank Christ,' said Ben.

The Bee Gees started to sing. 'Ah – ah – ah – ah – stayin' alive, stayin' alive. Ah – ah – ah …'

'Ah Jesus,' said Ben. 'I'm going.'

Pat grabbed Ben's arm.

'Hang on,' he said. 'We'll stay for one pint.'

They were glad they stayed. They were putting the pints to their mouths when the pub began to fill. It was great. There were lads from Dublin and lads from Liverpool. There were girls from Liverpool. The pub was full. The craic was good.

'I'm going to the jacks,' said Ben.

'Send us a postcard,' said Dave.

Ben went into the toilet.

And that, really, is where the story starts. In a jacks in Liverpool. Not *in* the jacks. At the door, just outside the jacks.

Six

They didn't miss Ben at first. They were talking to two girls.

'Where are you from, lads?' said one of the girls.

'Dublin,' said Dave.

'Oooh, we love Dublin,' said the girl. 'Don't we, Barb?'

'Yeah,' said Barb. 'Dublin is mad.'

'And we're mad too,' said the first girl. 'Tell the lads, Barb. We're mad.'

'We're mad,' said Barb.

'I'm Tracy, by the way,' said the first girl. 'And this is Barb.'

'All right, lads?' said Barb.

'She's mad,' said Tracy.

'So is she,' said Barb.

'We're both mad,' said Tracy.

'How mad?' said Dave.

'Mad as shite,' said Tracy. 'Isn't that right, Barb?'

'Madder,' said Barb.

'What's your names, lads?' said Tracy.

'Well,' said Dave. 'I'm Dave.'

'Are you mad, Dave?' said Tracy.

'A bit mad,' said Dave.

'You look mad,' said Tracy.

'Thanks,' said Dave.

'He looks mad,' said Tracy. 'Doesn't he, Barb?'

'Yes,' said Barb.

Tracy looked at Pat.

'Who are you then?' she said.

Pat gulped. Tracy really did look a bit mad. But she looked kind of *nice* mad. Kind of sexy mad. He liked her.

'I'm Pat,' said Pat.

'His name is Pat,' Tracy told Barb. 'He looks mad too.'

'Not as mad as Dave,' said Barb.

'No,' said Tracy. 'Dave is mad as shite. Aren't you, Dave?'

'I try my best,' said Dave.

So, that was it. Tracy liked Dave. Pat knew the story. He looked at Barb. She smiled at him. He liked her too. She wasn't as nice as Tracy. But she was nice.

'All right, Pat?' she said.

'I'm all right,' said Pat. 'Are you all right, Barb?'

'I'm all right,' said Barb.

'She's mad,' said Tracy.

So, that was it. It was Dave and Tracy, and Pat and Barb. Two lads and two girls, on a Saturday morning. Ben was in the jacks and they didn't miss him.

Dave grinned at Pat.

'I don't like your one much,' he said, very quietly.

Pat spoke with a Liverpool voice.

'I'm mad, Dave,' he said. 'Are you mad?'

'I'm mad, Pat,' said Dave.

'Are you over for the match, Dave?' said Tracy.

'Yes,' said Dave.

'I hate Liverpool,' said Tracy.

'I like it,' said Dave.

He nodded at the window of the pub. He nodded at the city outside.

'The team,' said Tracy. 'Not the city. I hate the football team.'

'Oh,' said Dave.

'I'm Everton,' she said.

Everton was the other Liverpool team.

'Oh,' said Dave.

'And so is my boyfriend,' said Tracy.

'Oh,' said Dave.

'He's gone to see Everton,' she said. 'They are playing away from home.'

She looked at Dave.

'And so am I,' she said.

'Nice one,' said Dave, to himself.

She spoke right into his ear. Her hair tickled his face.

'I'm mad, Dave,' she said. 'What do you think of that?'

'It makes me very happy,' said Dave.

Seven

The bar was packed. Dave looked at the clock on his mobile. It was twelve o'clock.

'Do you want a drink, Tracy?' he said.

'Vodka,' said Tracy.

'What do you want with it?' said Dave.

'More vodka,' said Tracy.

Dave laughed.

'I'm mad,' said Tracy. 'I told you, Dave.'

'Where's Ben?' said Pat.

'Who's Ben?' said Tracy.

'He's our pal,' said Pat. 'Where is he?'

'Over there,' said Dave.

'Where?' said Pat.

'I saw him a minute ago,' said Dave. 'Over at that door.'

It was more than an hour since Pat had seen Ben. He looked at where Dave had pointed.

'I don't see him,' he said.

'Don't worry,' said Dave. 'He's grand.'

Dave was trying to get the barman to look at him.

'Two pints of Bud!'

But the barman didn't hear him.

'Two pints of Bud!' Dave said again.

He said it ten times but the barman didn't look at him. He looked at every other face in the pub but not Dave's.

'I give up,' said Dave.

'Ah, Dave,' said Tracy. 'Let me try.'

27

She pushed past Dave.

'HEY!'

The barman looked at Tracy.

'Yes, love?' he said.

'Two pints of Bud and a vodka and Coke,' said Tracy. 'What about you, Barb?'

'Gin,' said Barb.

'Not gin, Barb,' said Tracy. 'It makes you sad.'

'I want gin,' said Barb.

'It's not dark yet, Barb,' said Tracy. 'It's still the morning.'

'I want gin,' said Barb.

She nodded at Pat.

'I need gin,' she said, very quietly.

'Do you not like him?'

'He's OK,' said Barb. 'But he's dead boring. All he talks about is football.'

'How's it going with Barb?' Dave asked Pat.

'Great,' said Pat. 'She's mad into the football.'

'Is that right, man?' said Dave.

'Yes,' said Pat.

'But Tracy said Barb hates football,' said Dave.

'Does she?'

'Yes,' said Dave. 'Her da dropped dead when Wayne Rooney got that goal against Arsenal three years ago.'

'Did he?'

'Yes,' said Dave. 'In front of the telly.'

'Was she there?' said Pat.

'He landed on her,' said Dave.

'Oh God,' said Pat.

'She likes dogs,' said Dave.

'Is that right?' said Pat.

'Yes,' said Dave. 'She's mad into dogs.'

'Thanks,' said Pat.

'No problem,' said Dave.

The barman gave Tracy the drinks. She gave Pat a pint of Bud, and a gin and tonic.

'The gin's for Barb,' she said.

'OK,' said Pat. 'Thanks.'

He went over to Barb.

'All right, Pat?' said Barb.

'All right, Barb,' said Pat.

He gave her the gin and tonic.

'Do you like dogs, Barb?' said Pat. 'I love them.'

Pat looked at Barb. He looked at the water come out of her eyes. She was crying.

'What?' he said.

'My dog,' she said.

'What?' he said again.

'My dog is dead!'

'Oh God,' said Pat.

He looked across at Dave.

Dave was smiling. He lifted his glass.

'Cheers, Pat,' he said.

Pat looked at Barb. She was still crying.

'Sorry about the dog,' he said. 'When did he die?'

'Yesterday,' said Barb.

She was crying when she said it. So it came out like this: 'Yes– yes– yes– yesterday.'

'What was his name?' said Pat.

Barb put her nose on Pat's chest.

'Ben,' she said.

Pat looked over Barb's head. He looked all over the pub.

Where was Ben?

Eight

Where was Ben?

'Our pal is called Ben,' Pat told Barb.

'What pal?' said Barb.

'The fella who came here with us,' said Pat.

'What fella?'

She wiped her nose on Pat's shirt.

'He's here,' said Pat.

'Where?' she said.

'I don't know.'

Pat looked at Dave.

'Where's Ben?' he shouted.

But Dave didn't answer. He was kissing Tracy.

'I can't see him,' Pat told Barb.

'And he's named after my dog,' said Barb. 'Is he?'

'Yes,' said Pat. 'No. Not really. It's just the same name, like.'

'Well,' said Barb. 'If he's as nice as my Ben, your pal must be lovely.'

'He is lovely,' said Pat.

But he didn't like saying that. It didn't sound right. And Ben wasn't lovely at all. He was an ugly muppet.

'He had lovely fur,' said Barb.

'He doesn't have any fur,' said Pat.

'My dog, Pat,' said Barb. 'He had fur.'

'Oh,' said Pat. 'Our Ben just has hair. On his head, like.'

Ah Jesus, where was Ben?

Pat looked all around him. The pub was packed. There was no room to move.

'I'll be back in a bit,' he told Barb.

Pat let go of Barb and tried to push

his way to the toilet. He saw Ben's head. But it wasn't Ben. It was some other ugly muppet.

Pat went into the toilet.

Tracy stopped kissing Dave.

'All right, Dave?' she said.

'All right, Tracy,' said Dave.

'Where's Pat, Barb?' said Tracy.

'He's gone to the bog,' said Barb.

'Are you all right, Barb, love?' said Tracy. 'Your eyes are all red.'

'I miss Ben,' said Barb.

'Oh good,' said Dave. 'You met Ben.'

'Her dog, Dave,' said Tracy. 'Poor Barb misses her dog.'

'Oh,' said Dave.

'Her dog died,' said Tracy. 'I told you.'

'I'm sorry for your troubles, Barb,' said Dave.

Pat was in the toilet. It was full of men. But none of them was Ben.

'Ben?' he called.

He hit the jacks door.

'Ben?'

'He's not in here, son,' said a voice on the other side of the door. 'I'm in here on my own.'

'Thanks,' said Pat.

'No problem,' said the voice. 'If he climbs out of the bog, I'll tell him you were looking for him.'

'Thanks,' said Pat again.

He went back out to the bar.

'Well, Dave,' said Tracy. 'Are you still going to the match?'

'What do you mean, Tracy?'

'You can come back to my flat,' said Tracy.

'Are Liverpool playing in your flat, Tracy?'

'No, Dave,' said Tracy. 'Not today.'

'Then I think I'll go to the match,' said Dave.

But he liked Tracy. A lot.

'I don't want to let the lads down,' he said.

He smiled at her.

'We can meet after the match,' he said.

Pat was beside Dave.

'I can't find Ben,' he said.

'He's over there,' said Dave.

'Where?' said Pat.

'I don't know,' said Dave.

'He's not here,' said Pat.

'He's fine,' said Dave. 'He's with a bird.'

'How do you know?' Pat asked.

'I don't know,' said Dave. 'I just think he is.'

'Why?'

'Because *I* am, Pat,' said Dave. 'And so are you. Go over to Barb. She misses you.'

'She misses her dog,' said Pat.

'You be her dog, Pat,' said Dave.

'All right, lads?' said Tracy.

'Ben is missing,' said Pat.

'He's not missing,' said Dave. 'He just isn't here.'

'Text him,' said Tracy.

'Good idea,' said Dave.

Pat took out his mobile phone.

Barb came over.

'All right, Pat?'

'I'm texting Ben,' said Pat.

'My dog?'

'No, Barb,' said Pat. 'My pal.'

'My Ben barked when he heard a text,' said Barb. 'The buzz, like. He went mad.'

'Ah, that's lovely,' said Dave.

'He was mad, Dave,' said Tracy. 'That dog was mad.'

'He loved Fatboy Slim,' said Barb.

'Is that right?' said Dave.

'I got him a Fat Boy Slim CD for Christmas,' said Barb.

'Did he like it?' said Dave.

'Yes, he did,' said Barb. 'But he liked the other one better.'

'OK,' said Dave.

Pat sent Ben a text. *Where r u?*

He held his mobile. He waited for Ben to text back. The pub was full and noisy. He didn't hear the text. But he felt it in his hand. He read it. *Do u have clean underpants?* It wasn't from Ben. It was from Pat's mother.

Barb looked at the text. *Do u have clean underpants?*

'Did Ben send that?' she said.

'No,' said Pat. 'My ma did.'

'Is she here too?' said Barb. 'With Ben?'

'No,' said Pat. 'She's in Dublin.'

'Hey, Pat,' said Dave. 'Did Ben text you?'

'No,' said Barb. 'His mam did.'

Pat wanted to run. He wanted to run out to the street. Barb was going to tell them about his underpants. He knew she was. She was mad.

But he liked her. He didn't run.

'She asked him if his kaks are clean,' said Barb.

'Nice one,' said Dave.

'Well, Barb,' said Tracy. 'You find out and text her back.'

They laughed. Pat did too.

Barb put her hand in Pat's back pocket. And Pat forgot about Ben for a while.

Nine

It was getting near to kick-off time.

Dave put Tracy's phone number into his phone. She got Dave's number. Pat got Barb's number. And she got Pat's.

'Come on,' said Dave to Pat. 'We'll be late for the match.'

'What about Ben?' said Pat.

It was an hour after Pat had sent Ben the text. Ben still hadn't sent one back.

'We'll see him there,' said Dave. 'He has his ticket.'

'OK.'

Dave kissed Tracy.

'See you later, Tracy,' he said.

'You never know, Dave, love,' said Tracy. 'I might wait for you.'

Barb kissed Pat.

'See you, Pat.'

'See you, Barb.'

'If I see Ben I'll tell him you've gone to the match,' said Barb.

'You don't know what he looks like,' said Pat.

'Sorry,' said Barb. 'I'm a bit drunk.'

'She's dead horny when she's drunk, Pat,' said Tracy. 'Aren't you, Barb?'

'Yes, I am.'

'She's mad.'

'I'm mad.'

'And horny,' said Tracy.

'And horny,' said Barb. 'But I miss Ben.'

She started to cry.

'Come on, for God's sake,' said Dave.

He grabbed Pat's jacket and they pushed through men and boys and women and girls. They got to the door. Pat felt the fresh, cold air.

They heard Tracy in the pub.

'She's horny and sad, lads!'

The door closed.

They were out on the street. Dave saw a taxi. He lifted his hand. The taxi stopped.

'Easy,' said Dave.

They both got in.

'All right, lads?' said the taxi driver.

'All right,' said Dave.

'Going to the match?' said the taxi driver.

'Yes,' said Dave.

'Waste of money,' said the driver. 'Liverpool are shite.'

'Will you take us anyway?' said Dave.

'All right, all right,' said the driver.

'All right,' said Dave.

It was the only thing they said in this town. All right.

'How long will it take?' said Dave.

'Ten minutes,' said the driver.

'All right,' said Dave.

'It's not far, lads,' said the driver.

'All right,' said Dave.

The driver looked at Dave.

'Are you taking the piss?' he said.

'No,' said Dave.

'All right,' said the driver.

'All right,' said Dave.

Pat sent Ben a new text. *Where d f r u?*

'I can't wait for this match, man,' said Dave.

'Yes,' said Pat.

They looked out the windows of the taxi. The streets were full of people in red jerseys and jackets. There were other people with red flags. They were near Anfield, where Liverpool played all their games.

'It's a dump,' said the taxi driver.

'All right,' said Dave.

The taxi stopped.

'Get out,' said the driver.

'Why?' said Dave. 'We're not there yet.'

'You were taking the piss.'

'I wasn't.'

'You were.'

'All right,' said Dave.

He opened his door. He got out. Pat did too.

'Hey,' said the driver. 'What about my money?'

'We don't want it,' said Dave. 'You can keep it.'

He ran. Pat ran after him. They ran and laughed.

They saw Anfield up the street. It wasn't far. People were walking up the middle of the street. There were no cars. The taxi driver wouldn't follow them. They stopped running.

'Time for a pint?' said Dave.

'No,' said Pat. 'I want to see if Ben is there.'

He heard his phone. It was a text.

'Speak of the devil,' said Dave. 'That's Ben.'

But it wasn't from Ben. It was from Barb. *I miss u. xxxxx B.*

Dave read the text.

'You're away there, man,' he said.

'And you and Tracy,' said Pat.

'A good day's work,' said Dave. 'And it's only half two.'

They were in the crowd now, all going to Anfield.

'Liver-pool! Liver-pool!'

It was great. It was exciting.

'Liver-pool! Liver-pool!'

They looked at the numbers on their tickets. They found the right gate. They were in. They were inside Anfield.

'Liver-pool! Liver-pool!'

'I'm hungry,' said Dave.

'Me too,' said Pat.

There was a chipper under the stand and a woman behind the counter.

'All right, lads?' she said.

'All right,' said Dave.

'What can I get you, lads?' she said.

'Two cheeseburgers and chips,' said Dave.

'What about Ben?' said Pat. 'He'll be hungry as well.'

'OK,' said Dave. 'Make that three cheeseburgers, Missus.'

'All right,' she said.

'All right,' said Dave.

They paid for the food and they

went up the steps. They found their seats.

No Ben.

'Where is he?' said Pat. 'The muppet.'

Dave's phone buzzed. It was a text. It wasn't from Ben. *I'm yours if they win*. It was from Tracy.

He showed the text to Pat.

'This is a great city,' he said. 'I'm moving here.'

'What if they lose?' said Pat.

'They won't,' said Dave.

'Where's Ben?' said Pat.

'He'll be here, man,' said Dave. 'I'm telling you.'

He bit into his burger.

'Jesus.'

'What's wrong?' said Pat.

'It's the burger,' said Dave.

'What about it?' said Pat.

Dave lifted the bun and looked at the meat.

'It's raw.'

'Thanks for telling me,' said Pat. 'I won't have to eat mine.'

'I'm going to be sick,' said Dave.

'How are the chips?' said Pat.

'Lovely,' said Dave.

He put five chips into his mouth. He forgot about the burger.

The stadium was filling up. Lines of people were coming up the steps and filling the seats. Pat and Dave looked for Ben. They hoped they'd see him in the line. But they didn't.

'Oh Jesus,' said Dave.

'What?' said Pat.

'I ate some of my burger,' said Dave.

'But you said it was raw,' said Pat.

'I forgot,' said Dave. 'I might as well finish it now. I'm going to die anyway.'

Most of the seats were full now.

'Liver-pool! Liver-pool!'

The seat beside Pat was empty. He

checked his phone. But there was no text from Ben.

'He's going to miss the match,' said Pat.

'There's still time,' said Dave. 'He's on his way.'

The music started. Before every game the crowd sang 'You'll Never Walk Alone'. It was great. All those voices singing at the same time. Pat joined in.

'Walk on,' he sang. 'Walk on!'

'Shut up,' said Dave.

The music ended. The crowd cheered. The teams ran onto the pitch. Liverpool were playing Chelsea that day. The crowd cheered as the Liverpool names were called out.

'Liver-pool! Liver-pool!'

And they booed when the Chelsea names were called out.

Everybody was standing now.

'Liver-pool! Liver-pool!'

Pat felt his phone buzz in his pocket. It was his mother again. *The match is on telly. Wave.*

The match started. Everybody sat down.

'What are you doing?' said Dave.

'Waving,' said Pat.

'Why?'

'I think I know someone over there,' said Pat.

His face was very red.

'Who?' said Dave.

But Liverpool had the ball and Dave forgot about Pat. All around them men were shouting.

'Give it to Stevie!'

'Give it a go!'

'Go back to bed!'

It was great. It was funny. But Pat missed Ben. He was worried. He was at the match and Ben might be in trouble. Big trouble. That was what Pat kept thinking.

Chelsea scored first. It was a penalty.

'No way was that a penalty!'

But it was a penalty. The Chelsea player, Frank Lampard, stepped up to the spot.

'He'll miss it,' said Dave.

But he didn't. They watched the ball hit the back of the net.

'Bastard.'

The stadium was very quiet. Dave heard his phone.

'Hello?'

'All right, Dave?'

It was Tracy.

'It's not looking good, Dave,' she said.

Then she was gone. The phone was dead.

The noise started again. The fans began to shout.

'Come on, lads!'

'All right, lads!'

'Liver-pool! Liver-pool!'

It was still early in the game. There was plenty of time for Liverpool to score. They were playing good football. They would score.

And they did.

'YES!'

It was a good goal. It was a great goal. It was the best goal Pat and Dave had ever seen.

'YESSSS!'

They stood up. They punched the air. They hugged. All around them the place went mad. Dave took out his phone. He found Tracy's number. He held up the phone in the air.

'Can you hear that, Tracy?' he said.

He turned off the phone and put it back in his pocket.

They all sat down again.

'Now we have a game of football,' said Pat.

But the good times only lasted three

minutes. Chelsea scored again. It was Damien Duff.

'At least he's Irish,' said Pat.

'Shut up,' said Dave.

'Where the hell is Ben?' said Pat.

'I don't care,' said Dave.

But he did care. It wasn't good.

Dave felt his phone in his pocket. It was Tracy. *Bye bye, Dave.*

He looked up from his phone just in time to see Chelsea score again.

The place was very quiet. Dave took his head out of his hands. He looked at Pat.

'Come on,' he said.

He stood up.

'Where are we going?' said Pat.

'To find Ben,' said Dave.

Pat followed Dave. They went down the steps and under the stand. They went out of the stadium and onto the street.

'What will we do?' said Pat.

'I don't know,' said Dave.

He took out his phone.

'I'll text him,' he said. 'Maybe he didn't get yours. I bet he's with a woman.'

'Do you really think that?' said Pat.

'No,' said Dave.

'If he was with a woman he'd text us,' said Pat.

Dave nodded.

'I know,' he said. 'He'd send us a photograph.'

He pressed the green button and sent his text. *Where r u?*

'Would you care about Ben if Liverpool were winning?' Pat asked Dave.

'No way,' said Dave.

They heard a cheer.

'Was that a goal?' said Pat.

'I don't know,' said Dave.

'Will we go back in?'

'No,' said Dave. 'Let's find Ben. And then we'll kick the crap out of him.'

Ten

'How will we find him?' said Pat.

'I don't know,' said Dave.

'There's a guard,' said Pat.

He pointed at a policeman on a horse.

'They don't have guards here,' said Dave. 'This isn't Ireland.'

'He's an English guard,' said Pat.

'Stop being thick,' said Dave.

'He's a cop,' said Pat. 'Yes?'

'Yes.'

'So let's tell him about Ben,' said Pat.

'OK,' said Dave.

They walked over to the cop on the horse.

'Excuse me,' said Pat.

'Yes, sir?' said the cop.

Pat looked behind him. It was the first time he had ever been called 'sir'.

'Are you talking to me?' he said.

'Yes, sir,' said the cop. 'How can I help you?'

'We can't find our friend,' said Pat.

He felt like an eejit. He sounded like a little boy who'd lost his mammy.

The cop looked down at him from the horse.

'Where did you lose him?' he said.

Pat looked at Dave.

'In the pub,' said Dave.

'What pub, sir?'

'The Bee Hive,' said Dave.

'Do you know it?' said Pat.

'Yes, sir.'

The cop looked down at Dave.

'You lost your friend in the Bee Hive, sir?'

'Yes,' said Dave.

'And what age is he?' said the cop.

'Twenty,' said Dave.

'A twenty-year-old man is lost in a pub,' said the cop.

He took his cap off. He looked down at Dave and Pat.

'Are you taking the piss, lads?'

'No,' said Pat. 'We did lose him. His name's Ben.'

'OK,' said the cop. 'OK.'

He put his cap back on.

'But,' he said, 'is he Irish too?'

'Yes,' said Pat. 'He's from Dublin. Like us.'

'So,' said the cop. 'An Irish lad is lost in a pub.'

He held up his walkie-talkie.

'Look, lads,' he said. 'If I report that I'll get the sack.'

'He's not in the pub,' said Pat.

'He's in another pub,' said the cop.

'We don't know,' said Pat.

The cop saw Pat's face. He saw that Pat was worried.

'Give it a few hours,' he said. 'He's a big boy. He's not missing yet. Go back to the Bee Hive. He might be looking for you.'

'He knows where we are,' said Pat. 'At the match.'

'You're not at the match, sir,' said the cop. 'And he might be.'

The cop tapped the horse with his heels. The horse walked away.

'He called me sir,' said Pat.

'Get a grip,' said Dave. 'Where will we go now?'

'What do you mean?' said Pat.

'Will we go back to the match?' said Dave. 'Or back to the Bee Hive?'

'The match,' said Pat.

They still had their tickets. They walked to the gate. There were three men coming out.

'Don't go in there, lads,' said one of the men. 'It's 4-1.'

'I'm going home to kill myself,' said the second man.

'Me too,' said the third one. 'I've nothing left to live for.'

Dave stopped. He looked at Pat.

'The Bee Hive?' he said.

'OK,' said Pat.

Eleven

The Bee Hive was nearly empty. This time the barman saw Dave.

'All right, lads?' he said.

'All right,' said Dave.

They sat at the bar.

'Well,' said Pat.

He looked around.

'Ben isn't here,' he said.

'And Tracy and Barb aren't here,' said Dave.

'What will we do?' said Pat.

'We'll find two other women,' said Dave.

'I mean about Ben,' said Pat.

'Oh,' said Dave. 'Him?'

They laughed.

'I know what we'll do,' said Dave. 'We'll get a map, right?'

'OK.'

'And we'll go down every street in this city.'

'OK.'

'And we'll look in every pub and restaurant.'

'OK.'

'How does that sound?' said Dave.

'Good,' said Pat. 'But I'm not drinking in all of them.'

'Don't be thick,' said Dave. 'We'll be looking for Ben.'

The barman put two pints in front of them.

'We'll just have these pints first,' said Dave.

'OK,' said Pat.

They picked up their glasses. They tapped them together.

'Cheers,' said Dave.

'Cheers,' said Pat.

And Tracy and Barb walked in.

Tracy looked at Dave.

'They lost, Dave,' she said.

'I know, Tracy,' said Dave.

'Sad,' said Tracy. 'Isn't it, Dave?'

'Yes, it is, Tracy,' said Dave.

'It could have been *so* good,' said Tracy.

'Ah well,' said Dave.

Tracy stood very close to Dave.

'We can pretend Liverpool won, Dave,' she said. 'Does that sound good?'

'No,' said Dave. 'It doesn't. But I can pretend it does.'

He kissed her.

'Look at the lovebirds, Pat,' said Barb.

'Yes,' said Pat.

'She's a bitch,' said Barb.

'Why?'

'She always gets the good-looking fellas,' said Barb.

'What about me?' said Pat.

'You're all right, Pat,' said Barb. 'But you're not as good looking as Dave.'

'Well, Barb,' said Pat. 'You're not as good looking as Tracy.'

'I know,' said Barb.

She started crying. She put her face into Pat's chest.

'I miss Ben *so* much,' she said.

'So do I,' said Pat.

He kissed her hair. She put her arms around him.

'Look at them,' said Tracy. 'The sluts.'

Twelve

If you think that Dave and Pat forgot about Ben, you are wrong.

They went looking for him. They went into thirty pubs but they only drank in sixteen of them. They went into twenty-seven restaurants but they only ate in two.

They were in a Chinese restaurant. It was eight o'clock. Pat and Barb had the chicken and sweetcorn soup. Dave had a spring roll. And Tracy had a very good idea.

'I'll text all my pals,' she said. 'I'll tell them to look out for Ben.'

'Top girl, Tracy,' said Dave. 'Great idea.'

It was a great idea. But it was also the start of a new problem. But they didn't know that yet.

'What does he look like?' said Tracy.

'Who?' said Pat.

'Ben,' said Tracy.

'Why?' said Pat.

'For the text,' said Tracy.

'He's an ugly muppet,' said Dave. 'Isn't he, Pat?'

'He's not that bad,' said Pat.

'Do you fancy him, Pat?' said Tracy.

'No,' said Pat. 'Get lost.'

'Leave Pat alone,' said Barb.

'What colour are his eyes?' said Tracy.

'I don't know,' said Pat.

'Yes, you do,' said Tracy.

'I don't,' said Pat. 'I don't care about stuff like that. Eyes and that.'

Pat was very red.

'They're blue,' said Dave.

'What?'

'Ben's eyes.'

'That's right,' said Pat.

'You said you didn't know,' said Tracy.

'Leave Pat alone,' Barb said again.

Barb was a bit angry with Tracy. Pat could see that. Barb liked Dave. But her hand was on Pat's leg. So Pat was happy.

But he wasn't really happy. How could he be? Ben was missing. His best friend. His oldest friend. The best man at his wedding, if he ever got married.

Tracy read her text. *Missing. A blue-eyed Irish muppet called Ben. Call if u meet him.*

'You have a way with words, Tracy,' said Dave.

'I have a way with lots of things, Dave,' said Tracy.

She sent the text to all the numbers in her phone book.

Pat was drunk. He kept forgetting about Ben. Then he remembered.

'What will we do?' he said.

'Well, I'm having the curry,' said Dave.

'About Ben,' said Pat.

'Oh,' said Dave. 'Him?'

But Pat didn't laugh this time.

Then he forgot. Then he was kissing Barb. Then he was eating sweet and sour chicken. Then he woke up. He must have fallen asleep.

'All right, Pat?'

Then he was in the toilet. He didn't remember going there. He washed his face. He felt better. He went back out to the restaurant.

They were gone. Dave and Tracy and Barb were gone.

But they weren't. He was looking the wrong way.

'Hey, Pat,' said Dave.

Pat went over to the table. He hit two tables on his way.

'Did you move?' said Pat.

He sat down. He missed the chair. He sat on Barb's lap.

'Yes, we moved,' said Dave. 'It was getting boring at the other table.'

'Ah, Pat, love,' said Barb. 'Get your elbow out of my curry.'

'Sorry,' said Pat.

He sat on his own chair.

'Where's my dinner?' he said.

'You ate it,' said Dave.

'Did I?'

'Yes,' said Dave.

'Was it nice?' said Pat.

'You ate it, man. Not me.'

They heard the sound of Tracy's phone.

'Another one,' she said.

She picked the phone off the table.

'No one has seen Ben yet,' she told Pat.

She looked at the latest text.

'Uh oh,' she said.

'What?' said Dave.

'It's my boyfriend.'

Pat turned around.

'Where?' he said.

'The text,' said Dave. 'What does he want?' he asked Tracy.

'He wants to know who Ben is,' she said. 'And he wants to know where I am.'

And that was the new problem. They were looking for Ben. And now Tracy's boyfriend was looking for them.

'Don't tell him where we are,' said Dave.

'I won't,' she said.

She put the phone back on the table.

'He'll kill you, Dave,' said Tracy.

'He's mad,' said Barb. 'Isn't he, Tracy?'

'That's right, Barb,' said Tracy. 'He's mad, Dave.'

'So what?' said Dave.

'He's really mad, Dave,' said Tracy. 'He's *really* mad.'

'Who's mad?' said Pat.

'Go back to sleep,' said Dave.

'He is so mad, Dave,' said Tracy.

'He's lovely,' said Barb.

And she started to cry.

'What's wrong with Barb?' said Pat.

'She's grand,' said Dave. 'The curry reminded her of her dog. That's all.'

'She used to go with my boyfriend,' Tracy told Dave.

'Is that right?'

'That's right,' said Tracy. 'But he broke it off with her.'

'Is that right?'

'That's right,' said Tracy. 'And sometimes she blames me for it.'

'Is that right?'

'That's right,' said Tracy. 'I don't know why.'

'What's his name?' said Dave.

'Basher,' said Tracy.

'Basher?' said Dave.

'I thought the dog's name was Ben,' said Pat.

'Go back to sleep,' said Dave.

He looked at Tracy.

'What's his real name?' he said.

'That's his real name,' said Tracy.

'Basher?'

'Yes,' said Tracy. 'You should meet his mum. She's mad too. Isn't she mad, Barb?'

Barb was still crying. She nodded.

'That's right,' she said.

She was looking down at her phone. She was texting Basher. Her old boyfriend. The man she still loved. She was telling him where they were.

Thirteen

Basher was called Basher because his mother sneezed. She had wanted to call the baby Sasha. But, just when she was telling the priest his name, she sneezed. The priest didn't hear her right. He put water on the baby's head and said, 'I name this child Basher.'

Everybody in the church laughed. And for the rest of his life Sasha was called Basher.

Basher wasn't a hard man. But, with a name like Basher, he had to act like a hard man. And Basher was a very good actor.

Basher walked into the restaurant.

'Good evening, Mister Basher.'

'Welcome, Mister Basher.'

'Everton lost again, Mister Basher. We are so sorry.'

People looked at Basher. People looked away from Basher. People stood up and nodded at Basher. People stood up and ran to the toilet. Basher was in the room. Everybody knew it.

Basher stood at the door. He looked for Tracy and Barb.

They weren't there.

Fourteen

Tracy and Barb were with Pat. They were on the street, outside a pub called the Perfect Crime. Pat was leaning against the wall. He was asleep. It was starting to rain.

Dave came out.

'Ben isn't in there,' he said. 'But it's very nice.'

He went back in.

'All right, Pat?' said Barb.

She shook Pat. He woke up. He looked around.

'Where's my bedroom?' he said.

'Come on,' said Barb.

She grabbed the skin at the back of his neck and pulled him into the pub. She did that with one hand. She texted Basher with the other hand.

It was a good pub. It wasn't too hot. The music was good. The drink was cheap. The barman was quick.

They all had a drink called a Mental. It was a mixture of brandy, vodka, gin, whiskey and a slice of lemon.

Pat was awake again. The sleep had done him good.

They sat at a high round table. They all picked up their glasses.

'Cheers.'

'Cheers.'

'Cheers.'

'Cheers.'

And Basher walked into the pub.

There was silence. Even the music stopped.

Basher walked over to the table. He walked very slowly. They looked at him. Everybody looked at him. Nobody spoke. Nobody even took a breath. Basher was in the house. And someone was going to die.

They all looked at Basher.

He walked slowly to the table.

'All right, Basher?' said Tracy.

Basher looked at Dave.

'Who are you?'

'Dave,' said Dave. 'Who are you?'

'Basher,' said Basher.

They stared at each other. Their noses were two inches apart. Their eyes never blinked. Barb felt sorry now. She wished she hadn't texted Basher. She didn't want a fight. She didn't want to see Dave bleed to death under the table.

Dave and Basher stared at each other.

'All right, Basher?' said Dave.

'All right, Dave,' said Basher. 'Same again, is it?'

He went up to the bar.

'I told you,' said Tracy. 'He's mad.'

Basher came back with five more Mentals.

Pat picked up his glass.

'Thanks, Rasher,' he said.

He laughed. And Basher hit him.

But not too hard.

They all lifted their glasses.

'Cheers.'

Fifteen

The knife cut across Dave's eyes. The pain was terrible. He put his hands to his face. He was awake.

It was the sun. It wasn't a knife. It was shining through the window into his eyes.

What window?

Dave sat up in the bed.

What bed? It wasn't the hotel room. He didn't even remember the hotel room. He didn't know where he was. He hadn't a clue. His head was killing him. His head was split open. His brain was falling out.

He heard a voice.

'Oh God.'

He looked down. There was a man beside him in the bed.

He jumped out of the bed. Where was he? Who was it?

He heard another voice.

'All right, Dave?'

Who was she?

He heard another voice. He looked behind him. There was a man on the floor, waking up. He knew this one. It was Pat.

'Where am I?' said Pat.

'I don't know,' said Dave.

'All right, Pat?' said the woman in the bed.

It was all coming back.

'You're Tracy,' said Dave.

'Well done, Dave,' said Tracy.

'Who's that?' said Dave.

He pointed at the man in the bed.

'That's Basher,' said Tracy.

'Where's Barb?' said Dave.

Pat stood up. He lifted his shirt off the floor. There was a woman's face under it.

'Is this her?' said Pat.

'Yes,' said Tracy. 'That's Barb.'

'She looks nice,' said Pat. 'Do we know her?'

'Yes,' said Dave. 'We do.'

Pat looked at the window.

'Why is it bright?' he said. 'It hurts.'

'It must be morning,' said Dave.

'Where are we?' said Pat.

'Liverpool.'

'Liverpool?' said Pat.

'Yes,' said Dave. 'It's Sunday morning.'

Pat looked around the room.

'Where's Ben?' he said.

'We lost him,' said Dave. 'Remember?'

'Oh,' said Pat. 'It's coming back. Is this the hotel?'

Tracy spoke. She sat up.

'This is Basher's flat,' she said. 'He's going to kill you when he wakes up.'

Dave remembered.

'But he asked us here,' he said.

'He won't remember.'

'I thought we found Ben last night,' said Pat.

'No,' said Dave.

'He might be at the hotel,' said Pat.

They looked at each other.

'Let's go,' said Dave.

He was wide awake now. And so was Pat. They had to find Ben.

They got dressed quickly. They put on their shoes. They ran to the door.

Dave stopped. He looked at Tracy. Basher and Barb were still asleep.

'Two questions before I go,' he said.

'Fire away, Dave,' said Tracy.

'Did anything happen between me and you?'

'Do you not remember?'

'No.'

'Then I'm not telling.'

Tracy looked good in the bed.

'Second question,' said Dave.

He made sure Pat was outside. Then he nodded at Basher.

'Did anything happen between me and him?' he said.

'Do you really want to know, Dave?' said Tracy.

'Yes,' said Dave.

Tracy opened her mouth.

'I mean no,' said Dave.

Tracy smiled.

'Bye, Dave.'

'Bye.'

He ran down the stairs and out to the street. He met Pat there. They ran. They looked for a taxi. They kept running. There was no one on the street. No cars and no people. No taxis. They ran.

Sixteen

They didn't find Ben.

They went to the police.

They stayed in Liverpool for a week. They looked everywhere. And the police looked.

They phoned Ben's ma. They talked to his da. His family came to Liverpool. They were on the news. Asking for Ben. Asking for information.

They texted him all the time. *Where r u?*

They hoped.

He never answered.

They spoke to the police. They tried to explain. The police spoke to Tracy and Barb. They spoke to Basher.

Dave and Pat stayed another week.

They never found Ben.

They went home to Dublin.

Seventeen

There was no funeral. There was no body.

It went on for months.

Dave and Pat stopping going to Ben's house. His ma and da were angry. They blamed Dave and Pat. They never said anything. But Dave and Pat knew.

They stopped going to the local pub. It was the pub where they had watched Liverpool win the European Cup. People went silent when Pat and Dave walked in. They nodded and said hello. But they looked at Pat and Dave like there was something wrong with them. Something bad. So they stopped going.

They stopped going anywhere. They didn't like talking about Ben. There was nothing new to say. And they didn't like *not* talking about Ben.

There was Hallowe'en, and no Ben. There was Christmas, and no Ben.

Where r u?

Dave and Pat didn't really meet any more. It was easier that way.

Dave didn't sleep. He didn't like closing his eyes. He didn't like the dreams. He didn't eat much. He was never hungry. His skin was very dry. His gums bled when he brushed his teeth. He was very thin.

His mother cried.

She put the football on the telly but Dave didn't watch it.

His mobile phone was always on. He always had it in his fist.

Where r u?

Pat left his job. He sold computers in a shop. But he didn't want to talk to people any more. He didn't want to talk at all. To anyone.

His girlfriend broke it off with him.

Her name was Lisa. She looked at him while she talked.

'Pat?'

'What?'

'Did you hear what I said?' she said.

'Yes,' he said.

'You didn't,' she said. 'What did I say?'

'Em …'

'I said I can't go on like this,' said Lisa.

'Like what?' said Pat.

'Ah, stop it,' said Lisa. 'You *know*.'

Pat said nothing. He looked at his socks.

'I know,' said Lisa. 'You've lost Ben and that.'

'Leave Ben out of this,' said Pat.

He said it loud. He was angry.

'Forget it,' said Lisa.

She stood up.

'See you,' she said.

She walked out of the café, onto Talbot Street. Pat didn't look at her. He didn't care.

But he did care. When she was gone he cared. But he didn't do anything. He didn't run after her. He didn't know what to do or what to say.

It was easier if he was alone.

He didn't look for other work. He stayed in bed for most of the day. He stayed in his room. Like Dave, he kept his mobile phone on.

Where r u?

He kept it on until he had no money left for credit. Then he threw it under the bed.

His mother was sick with worry. This wasn't her Pat. This wasn't her funny son who never sat still. This was a stranger.

She knocked on Pat's door.

She was afraid he was going to kill himself. She was afraid he had already killed himself.

She knocked again.

'Patrick?' she said.

There was no answer.

'Patrick?'

She opened the door. She did it slowly. She was frightened. It was dark.

He was sitting on the side of the bed. He was looking at the floor.

She went to him. She held his head.

'Pat, love,' she said. 'We'll have to do something about this.'

She felt his head move. He was nodding.

'I miss him,' he said.

'I know you do,' said his ma.

'I feel like I killed him,' said Pat.

'You didn't,' she said.

'I know,' he said. 'I know that. But it's how I feel. I can't help it.'

He had a shower. He got dressed. He ate his dinner with the rest of the family. He watched a bit of telly. He went to bed. He got up the next morning at the same time as everyone else. He did this every morning.

He got a new job.

He found his mobile phone under his bed. He sat on the bed. He sent a text to Ben.

Where r u?

He phoned Lisa.

'All right?'

'Pat?' she said.

'I'm sorry,' he said. 'For – you know.'

'That's OK,' she said. 'How are you anyway?'

'Grand,' he said. 'I'm better.'

'Good,' she said.

'Are you doing anything tonight?' he said.

'God, Pat,' she said. 'Did no one tell you?'

'Tell me what?' he said.

But he knew.

'I'm going with someone else,' said Lisa.

'Oh,' said Pat.

'You don't know him.'

'OK,' said Pat. 'Well, bye.'

'Bye, Pat,' she said. 'Look after yourself.'

'OK,' he said.

'Phone Dave,' she said.

'I don't want to go with Dave,' said Pat.

He heard her laugh. That made him feel good, then bad.

'Phone him,' she said. 'I saw him yesterday. He doesn't look good.'

'OK,' said Pat. 'Bye.'

He stood up. He put the phone in his pocket.

He took it out again. He was going to phone Dave.

The phone rang.

He jumped. He looked at the screen. It was Dave.

'Pat?'

'I was just phoning you,' said Pat.

'He texted me,' said Dave.

'What?'

'Ben,' said Dave. 'He sent me a text.'

'When?'

'Just now.'

Pat sat on the bed.

'You're sure?' he said.

'Yes,' said Dave.

'What did it say?' said Pat.

'"I'm OK."'

'Are you at home?' said Pat.

'Yes,' said Dave.

'I'll come over,' said Pat.

'OK.'

Pat stood up. The phone was still in

his hand. It buzzed – he felt it. He heard it.

He looked at the screen.

He opened the text.

I'm OK.

It was from Ben.

Eighteen

They both looked at Dave's phone.

'OK,' said Dave. 'Here goes.'

He phoned Ben. He held the phone to his ear.

'Anything?' said Pat.

Dave shook his head. He kept listening.

He looked bad. He was very thin. His clothes were dirty. There were red spots across his forehead.

He took the phone down.

'No answer,' he said.

He turned it off.

They said nothing for a while. They were in Dave's bedroom.

'He's out there,' said Pat.

'That's right,' said Dave.

'Maybe someone has his phone,' said Pat.

'No,' said Dave. 'It's Ben. I know it.'

Pat nodded.

'The muppet,' he said.

'He's out there, man.'

'That's right,' said Pat.

He looked at Dave.

'You look shite, by the way,' he said.

'Thanks,' said Dave. 'I'm catching up with you.'

Pat stood up.

'This place stinks,' he said.

He opened Dave's bedroom window. He stuck his head out.

'Oh, thank Jesus.'

He took his head back in.

'Put on a clean shirt,' he said. 'We'll go to the pub.'

Nineteen

They phoned Ben every day. They met after work. They used Dave's phone one night and Pat's phone the next night.

Ben didn't answer.

They sent him more texts.

Where r u?

How r u?

Happy birthday. Having a pint 4 u.

This went on for more than a month.

They got one text back.

I'm OK.

They phoned him when they read it. He didn't answer.

It was bad. They needed to hear his voice. They couldn't rest. They couldn't relax until they heard him. But the text was better than nothing. *I'm OK*.

They were Dave and Pat again. And, sometimes, when they were together, it felt like Ben was with them. *I'm OK*.

One night in the pub, Pat even bought three pints.

'God,' he said. 'Look what I'm after doing.'

'What?' said Dave.

'I bought a pint for Ben as well.'

He put the extra pint on a beer-mat, like there was someone there to drink it.

They tapped their glasses against the extra glass.

'Cheers.'

'Cheers.'

Dave's phone rang. He put it to his ear.

He heard the voice.

'All right?'

Pat looked at Dave's face. He went white, very quickly.

Dave spoke.

'Ben?'

'How's it going?'

It was Ben. It was definitely Ben.

Dave looked at Pat. He nodded. He moved over so Pat could sit beside him. Pat put his ear close to the phone.

'Where are you?' said Dave.

'Africa,' said Ben.

'Africa?'

'Yes.'

'How did you get there?' said Pat.

'It's a long story,' said Ben.

'What's it like there?'

'Big,' said Ben. 'There's loads of mountains and trees and stuff.'

He told them how he got there.

'I was kidnapped.'

'Kidnapped?' said Pat.

'Yes,' said Ben. 'By a woman.'

He told them how it happened. He went to the toilet in the Bee Hive. He met a woman on his way back. They got talking. He woke up in Africa.

'Just like that?' said Dave.

'I was really drunk,' said Ben. 'Remember?'

'That drunk?'

'She put something in my drink.'

'And you woke up in Africa?'

'That's right,' said Ben.

'How long were you asleep?' said Pat.

'I don't know,' said Ben. 'A few days.'

'But that was months ago,' said Dave. 'Nearly a year.'

'Yeah,' said Ben. 'Sorry.'

'Why didn't you phone us, man?'

'I was kind of busy,' said Ben.

'Busy!' Dave yelled. 'Busy? I'll break your head when I catch you.'

'Shut up and I'll tell you,' said Ben.

'OK,' said Dave. 'Are you coming home?'

'No,' said Ben.

'Why not?'

'It's great here,' said Ben.

'Why?'

'I'm in a cult,' said Ben.

'A cult?' said Dave.

'That's right,' said Ben.

'What sort of a cult?' said Pat.

'It's called the United Church of Love,' said Ben.

'Where did you join it?'

'In the Bee Hive,' said Ben. 'Outside the jacks. It's great.'

'How come?' said Dave.

'It's all about love,' said Ben.

'What do you mean?' said Dave.

'We ride one another,' said Ben.

'What?' said Pat. 'All day?'

'More or less,' said Ben. 'But we grow a few crops as well.'

'Ah well,' said Dave. 'You have to eat.'

'That's why I didn't phone you,' said Ben. 'It takes a bit of getting used to. Sorry.'

'How many women?'

'Twenty-two,' said Ben.

'Jesus,' said Pat. 'How many men?'

'Just me and another fella,' said Ben.

'No wonder you didn't phone us,' said Dave.

'Sorry again,' said Ben.

'No problem,' said Dave.

'Can we join?' said Pat.

'That's the thing,' said Ben. 'That's the only rule. You can't ask to join. You have to be asked.'

'And you were asked?' said Pat.

'That's right,' said Ben. 'Outside the jacks.'

'You lucky bastard,' said Dave.

'Thanks,' said Ben.

Dave and Pat were laughing.

'Look it,' said Ben. 'I have to go. Good luck.'

He was gone.

And that's it. That's the end of the story.

Ben is still in Africa. He phones his ma every week. He phones the lads. He texts them all the time.

Happy Xmas.

Did Liverpool win?

I'm on the job.

They text him back. He's thousands of miles away but it doesn't feel like that. They are The Lads again. He's having a great time and they are happy for him.

He'll come home some day. Or Pat and Dave might go to Africa. They'd like that.

When Pat goes to the toilet in a pub, he always stops when he comes out. He waits for a minute. And he smiles at all the women. Just in case.

OPEN DOOR SERIES

TRADE/CREDIT CARD ORDERS TO:
CMD, 55A Spruce Avenue,
Stillorgan Industrial Park,
Blackrock, Co. Dublin, Ireland.
Tel: (+353 1) 294 2560
Fax: (+353 1) 294 2564

TO PLACE PERSONAL/EDUCATIONAL
ORDERS OR TO ORDER A CATALOGUE
PLEASE CONTACT:
New Island, 2 Brookside,
Dundrum Road, Dundrum,
Dublin 14, Ireland.
Tel: (+353 1) 298 6867/298 3411
Fax: (+353 1) 298 7912
www.newisland.ie